Gloria Chipmunk, Star!

by JOAN LOWERY NIXON
Pictures by GEOFFREY HAYES

SCHOLASTIC BOOK SERVICES

NEW YORK • TORONTO • LONDON • AUCKLAND • SYDNEY • TOKYO

ISBN 0-590-31920-5

12 11 10 9 8 7 6 5 4 3 2 1   2   1 2 3 4 5 6/8

Printed in the U.S.A.   07

To Eileen,
well on her way to becoming a star

Chapter One

Gloria Chipmunk tied a yellow ribbon around one ear and climbed on her parents' bed. She hopped up and down trying to see herself in the big mirror on the wall.

"Oh, Gloria!" she said, clapping her hands. "Today you will be a star!"

She tap-danced into the kitchen and climbed into her chair. Her little brother, Tippy, banged his spoon on his high chair and made a face at her.

Gloria didn't mind. "Mother!" she said. "Today is the play our class is giving for the rest of the school! Today I will be a star!"

"But, Gloria," her mother said, putting some buttered toast on a plate, "I thought your part was very small."

"An actress has to start somewhere," Gloria said. "Our teacher, Miss Beaver, told us that it's not the size of the part that's important. It's what we put into it."

Her mother patted Gloria's head. "Gloria," she said, "I've had some bad news."

"What is it?" Gloria asked.

"Your grandmother is ill," her mother said. "It's not serious, but she needs me to take care of her. I'll have to leave in a few minutes. I can't even wait until the baby-sitter gets here."

"What baby-sitter?" Gloria wanted to know.

Her mother sighed. "Mrs. Porcupine. I know she complains that noisy youngsters set her quills on edge, but she's the only one I could find to take care of Tippy while I'm away. All of our friends and relatives are off with your father, gathering nuts in the North Woods."

Gloria's nose twitched. "I have to be in the play, Mother!"

"Of course you'll be in the play," her mother said. "Just be a good girl and take care of your little brother until Mrs. Porcupine gets here."

She picked up her purse, kissed Gloria and Tippy goodbye, and went out the door.

"I have to get to school!" Gloria said. She hoped Mrs. Porcupine would hurry.

When the knock on the door came, it wasn't Mrs. Porcupine. A dusty mole squinted at Gloria.

He said, "Mrs. Porcupine can't come.
She has aches in her back and pains in her
toes. Goodbye."

"Oh, no!" Gloria cried. The mole shuffled off. "What am I going to do?" Gloria walked back and forth, trying to think.

Tippy came to the door. "Where are you going, Gloria?" he asked. "I want to go, too."

"That's it!" Gloria said. She smiled at her brother. "How would you like to be in the second grade with me today? You could watch the play."

Tippy looked away.

"It's *The Sleeping Beauty*," Gloria said, trying to interest him. "And I play a small but very important part. I come in and tell the King, 'I have searched the castle and thrown out all the spindles, so the princess will not prick her finger.' "

"I want a cookie," Tippy said.

"If you go to school with me, I'll bring home a library book and read it to you."

Tippy looked at Gloria carefully. Then he said, "Okay."

Gloria washed his face and put on his new sweater. Then she jumped up and down once more on her parents' bed, so she could see herself in the mirror.

"Gloria!" she said. "You look just like a star!"

Chapter Two

Gloria held her little brother's paw on the way to school. "You'll sit with me in my desk and be very, very quiet," she told Tippy.

Mary Squirrel, Gloria's best friend, met her at the crossroads. "You can't take your little brother to school," she said. "They'll send you home."

"I have to be in that play," Gloria said.

Mary shrugged. "Most of us think it's a dumb play. We all know the story of *The Sleeping Beauty*. There's nothing exciting about hearing it all again."

"I think it's exciting," Gloria said. "I like being an actress."

The school was deep inside the grove of oaks in the hollow. Just as they arrived, the first bell rang.

"Quick!" Gloria said. "Let's go in the side door so no one will notice us."

She hurried into the room with Tippy, and lifted him onto the seat beside her. He was so small he couldn't see over the top of her desk.

Some of the children stared and giggled.

"What are you trying to do, Gloria?" Rodney Possum asked.

BE SURE
TO PUT
THE BOOKS
BACK WHERE
THEY
BELONG

"Shhh," Gloria said. "I brought my brother to see me act in the play, but it's a secret."

Miss Beaver came into the room. She smiled at the class. Everyone sat up straight and smiled at Miss Beaver. "This morning we will give our play," she said.

Some of them groaned. But Gloria sat up even straighter, and her nose twitched.

"First," Miss Beaver said, "I'll call the roll and make sure everyone is here."

"I want a cookie," Tippy said.

Rodney Possum snorted. Some of the others laughed.

Miss Beaver peered over her glasses at Gloria. "Did you say something, Gloria?" she asked.

"I want a cookie," Tippy said again.

"Is there someone in your seat with you?" Miss Beaver said.

"My little brother, Tippy," Gloria said in a brave voice. "He came to watch me act in the play."

"Oh, dear," Miss Beaver said. "You know our school rule, Gloria. If we let you bring your brother to school, tomorrow many more little brothers and sisters would be brought to school. You'll have to take him home."

"But then I won't be able to be in the play, because I have to take care of him today," Gloria said.

Miss Beaver looked sad. "I'm sorry," she said. "But the rule is the rule. You'll have to take your little brother home."

Chapter Three

Gloria took Tippy's paw and led him out of the classroom into the hallway. She would have to report to the office. Then she would have to take Tippy home. She felt awful, but she was not going to cry!

"I'm going to be in that play!" Gloria said. "Listen, Tippy, I'll bring home two books to read to you. All you have to do is be quiet. When the lady in the office talks to you, don't say a word."

"Okay," Tippy said.

"Good," Gloria said.

She took Tippy into the office. It smelled of chalk and ink and sunshine coming through the window.

"Here is a little boy who doesn't know where his mother is," Gloria said to Mrs. Fox, who sat behind the desk.

Mrs. Fox smiled at Tippy. "What a sweet little boy," she said. "What is your name, little boy?"

Tippy didn't say a word.

"I'm going to be in a play," Gloria said to Mrs. Fox. "It's a small part, but Miss Beaver says it's what we put into it that counts."

Gloria patted her yellow ribbon. "When the play is over I'll come back. Maybe I can help you find this little boy's mother."

"I want a cookie, Gloria," Tippy said.

"This little boy knows you," Mrs. Fox said. She looked carefully at Gloria and then at Tippy. "Is he your brother?"

"Yes," Gloria said softly.

"Oh, my. You'll have to take him home. You know he can't stay in school," Mrs. Fox said.

Tippy began to swing back and forth on Gloria's paw. "But I want to be in that play," Gloria managed to say as she tried to hang on to Tippy.

"I'm sorry, Gloria," Mrs. Fox said, "but we have to obey the rules."

Gloria carried her little brother out of the office into the hallway and put him on his feet. "I'm going to take care of you, Tippy," she said. "But I'm also going to be in that play! What am I going to do?"

"Give me a cookie," Tippy said.

"Where would I get a cookie?" Gloria said.

She looked up and down the hallway. No one was in sight. Everyone was in class. She could hear the buzzing of voices that came from the row of closed doors.

At this end of the hall were the first, second, and third grade classrooms. At the very end of the hall was the kindergarten.

Gloria smiled. "Tippy," she said, "would you like to be in kindergarten?"

"No," Tippy said.

"It's very nice in kindergarten," Gloria said. "There are games to play with and paints to paint with. And if you go to kindergarten today I'll bring home three books to read to you."

"No," Tippy said.

"But best of all, every morning the kindergarten teacher gives all the boys and girls milk and cookies," Gloria said.

Tippy thought a moment. "Okay," he said.

"Good," Gloria said. "Now, remember. You have to be quiet. When the teacher talks to you, don't say a word."

"Okay," Tippy said.

Chapter Four

Gloria led Tippy down the hall to the very end. She opened a door and went inside.

It had been two years since Gloria had been in kindergarten, but the room was just as big as she remembered it. It was bright and colorful, with paintings hanging on the walls.

And Mrs. Bear was still there with her cheerful smile and her nice, big lap that could hold half a dozen youngsters at once.

Mrs. Bear was giving cartons of milk to the boys and girls. "How nice to see you, Gloria!" she said. "How you've grown!"

"Thank you," Gloria said. She patted her yellow ribbon. "I'm going to be in *The Sleeping Beauty* play today."

"Lovely," Mrs. Bear said. "We're coming to see the play. Are you one of the fairy godmothers?"

"No," Gloria said. "I have a small part, but Miss Beaver says it's what we put into the part that counts."

"Very wise," Mrs. Bear said. "But why aren't you in class? Who is this with you?"

"This is a new boy who is coming to kindergarten," Gloria said.

Mrs. Bear looked surprised. "He seems very young. Where is his mother?"

"She couldn't come," Gloria said.

"I don't understand it," Mrs. Bear said. "I should think Mrs. Fox would have brought him, or at least sent a note from the office."

Tippy began to squirm and swing from Gloria's paw again.

Gloria said quickly, "Since this little boy is coming to kindergarten today, could he have milk and cookies, too?"

Tippy looked at the tray and scowled. "They don't have cookies, Gloria," he said.

Mrs. Bear studied Tippy. Then she said, "Gloria, I have an idea that this is your little brother. Am I right?"

Oh, why couldn't Tippy have kept quiet? "Yes," Gloria said. "I have to take care of him today, but I want to be in the school play. I thought I could leave him here in the kindergarten until the play is over."

Tippy began to jump up and down. "I want a cookie!" he said.

Mrs. Bear looked sad. "I'm sorry, Gloria. I'd like to help you, but I can't. You'll have to take him home. You know the school rules."

Gloria led Tippy out into the hallway. She shut the door.

"Tippy," she said. "I have to take care of you, but I also have to be in that play! I'm going to think very hard! There must be some way I can do both!"

Chapter Five

The bell in the hallway rang, and Gloria turned to Tippy. "In just five minutes everyone will go to the auditorium," she said.

She thought a moment, then smiled. "Tippy! There's a baby buggy in the play, right in the middle of the stage. It's decorated in colored paper, and it's the bed for the pretend baby princess! I can hide you in the baby buggy, and then I can be in the play!"

"No," Tippy said.

"Tippy, if you hide in the baby buggy and are very quiet, I'll bring home four books to read to you."

"No," Tippy said.

"And I'll ask Mama to make lots of cookies, and I'll give all of mine to you."

"Okay," Tippy said.

Gloria took his paw and ran with him down the hall and into the auditorium. She helped him up the steps to the stage and lifted him high up into the baby buggy.

"Get under the blanket," she said. "And be very quiet, Tippy. Don't say a word."

"Okay," Tippy said.

The doors to the auditorium opened, and Miss Beaver's class marched in. Miss Beaver was surprised when she saw Gloria.

"Someone is taking care of Tippy," Gloria said. "I can be in the play."

"Fine," Miss Beaver said. She clapped her hands. "All you actors and actresses get in your places! The rest of the class can sit in the back rows of seats."

Gloria hurried to stand off the stage, behind the curtain. She patted her yellow hair ribbon. She hoped Tippy would be quiet!

Rodney Possum was the King. He put on a gold paper crown and fastened a robe around his neck. It was made from his mother's old red tablecloth. "Hurry!" he said to Lucy Raccoon, who was the Queen.

Lucy quickly put on her gold crown and stood next to Rodney at one side of the stage.

The other classes marched into the auditorium. Gloria could hear the shuffle of their feet and the scraping of chairs, and once in a while a giggle and a teacher saying, "Shh!"

The curtain opened, and the play began. Mary Squirrel, the first fairy godmother, came on stage. She had silver paper stars on the tips of her ears, and she carried a flower. Gloria was happy that her friend looked so beautiful.

Mary looked into the baby buggy, backed off, and tripped over her feet. She picked herself up, made a face, and said, "I wish grace and wisdom for the baby princess."

The second fairy godmother, Alicia Rabbit, came in waving her flower. Mary poked her in the ribs and nodded toward the baby buggy.

"Huh?" Alicia whispered.

Miss Beaver cleared her throat loudly, and Alicia quickly said, "I wish good health and joy for the baby princess."

The baby buggy began to wiggle.

The next fairy godmother, Dorothy
Porcupine, peeked into the buggy and said,
"I wish beauty and — hah, hah! Beauty and
— hah, hah, hah!" Dorothy giggled until
Mary rapped her on the nose with her
flower.

The baby buggy began to shake.

Lettie Groundhog rushed onto the stage waving her arms and looking angry. "I am the fairy godmother you didn't invite to the party!" she shouted. "And my wish for the princess is this...When she is sixteen she will prick her finger on a spindle and die!"

Gloria was excited. Soon it would be time for her part!

The King and Queen pretended to cry, but in came the last fairy godmother, Ophelia Skunk. "Don't worry," she said. "I'll change the spell. The princess will only fall asleep."

The buggy began to bounce and rock. Up and down Tippy jumped, trying to see out of it. "I want a cookie!" he shouted.

Everyone on stage stopped and stared at Tippy.

"Oh, no!" Gloria whispered. She had hoped with all her might that Tippy would behave himself. This was terrible! What if the audience booed? Rodney was staring at Tippy with his mouth open. He had forgotten his lines!

Gloria lifted her chin and took a deep breath. There was only one thing she could do to try to save the play.

Chapter Six

Gloria whirled onto the stage and tap-danced to the baby buggy. She smiled her biggest smile at the audience.

"I have searched the castle and thrown out all the spindles, so the princess will not prick her finger!" Gloria cried.

Tippy jumped up in the buggy again. "I want a cookie, Gloria," he shouted.

"Ah ha! I see that the princess is already under some kind of an evil spell," Gloria said. She threw a dazzling smile to the audience. "Well, it so happens that I am also a good fairy godmother in disguise, so I shall remove the evil spell."

Someone in the audience giggled.

Quickly Gloria grabbed Tippy and tap-danced across the stage and behind the curtain. She never forgot for a second to smile at the audience.

For a moment it was quiet. Then everyone began to laugh and applaud.

"I can't believe it!" Gloria cried happily. "No one is angry. Everyone likes what I did!" Just to make sure, she tap-danced across the stage to the other side, still carrying Tippy, and still smiling brightly at the audience.

When the cheering died down, the play continued. Gloria sat in the back row, holding Tippy, enjoying every moment.

"It was a bit unusual," Miss Beaver said later, peering over her glasses at Gloria. "But I must admit you did make the most of your part."

"It was the best *Sleeping Beauty* I ever saw," Mary said.

When Mother came home that afternoon, Gloria had Tippy and the four library books on her lap.

"Good news!" Mother said. "Grandmother is feeling much better." She kissed them both. "Tell me what you did today."

"We were in a play," Tippy said. "Mary hit everybody with a flower, and nobody gave me any cookies!"

"Mrs. Porcupine couldn't come, so I took Tippy to school," Gloria said quickly. "We were both in the play."

Mother hugged her. "How clever of you, Gloria," she said. "I'll bake Tippy some cookies, but first I want you to tell me all about what you and Tippy did in the play."

"It was a wonderful play," Gloria said. "Tippy was the baby princess." She reached up and patted her yellow ribbon. "And I — Oh, Mother, I was a *star!*"